Disney · PIXAR

TOY STORY 2

Disney
PRESS

New York

The evil Emperor Zurg appeared on the TV screen and fired at Buzz Lightyear.

"Oh, no!" Rex moaned. He had lost his favorite Buzz Lightyear video game . . . again!

The other toys tried to cheer him up—all except Woody. He was too busy getting ready to go to Cowboy Camp with Andy.

But at the last moment, disaster struck! Woody's arm ripped
while he and Andy were playing with Buzz.

There was no time to repair Woody, so Andy had to leave
without him.

Andy's mom put Woody on the mending shelf. There, Woody met Wheezy the squeaky penguin, one of Andy's old toys. Just then, Andy's mom reached up and took Wheezy from the shelf. She wanted to put him in their yard sale.

"Goodbye, Woody!" Wheezy called as he disappeared downstairs.

"I'm going to rescue Wheezy!" Woody announced, and he whistled for Buster, Andy's puppy. The two of them raced outside and grabbed Wheezy.

But as they headed back for the house, Woody's arm tore again and he tumbled to the ground. A greedy toy collector named Al was at the yard sale, and when he saw Woody he picked him up and ran to his car. The other toys watched in horror from the window as Al drove off with Woody.

Al took Woody to his apartment and locked him in. Woody looked around for a way to escape, but instead he found a floppy little horse called Bullseye and a friendly cowgirl called Jessie.

"Let's show him who he really is!" said an old prospector doll in a box.

Jessie turned on the TV. Woody was amazed as he watched the show, *Woody's Roundup!* starring Jessie, the Prospector, Bullseye . . . and Sheriff Woody!

Woody couldn't believe it. He had once been a television star, and now he was the last piece in a valuable toy collection.

"Al is selling us all to a museum in Japan," explained the Prospector.

Meanwhile, back at Andy's house, the clever toys had figured out that Al was the owner of the local toy store. That night, the toys decided to rescue their friend.

They went out to the rooftop. Slinky Dog held on with his paws as, one by one, Rex, Hamm, and Buzz used his coils to bungee jump to the ground.

"To Al's Toy Barn . . . and beyond!" Buzz shouted bravely. Then he led the way down the street. The friends walked on through the night. As the sun rose, they came to a busy main road . . . and spotted Al's Toy Barn.

"We have to get across!" Buzz shouted.

The toys each picked up a traffic cone and dashed into the busy road. "Drop!" Buzz yelled and hid beneath his cone. A truck swerved to miss them, spilling its load of concrete pipes.

"Go!" cried Buzz.

Ignoring the honking horns and screeching brakes around them, the toys made it safely inside the Toy Barn.

At Al's apartment, Woody sat with Jessie. His arm had been repaired and he looked brand new. "I'm all ready to go home to Andy now!" he cried.

"I belonged to a little girl once," Jessie said sadly. "She played with me every day, until she grew up. Then she gave me away. Even the greatest kids outgrow their toys. Listen, Woody, if you stay with us, you'll be remembered forever."

"Maybe you're right," Woody said quietly. "I think I'll stay after all."

Inside the Toy Barn, Buzz looked up at an amazing display of new Buzz Lightyear toys. Each one was wearing a super-utility pack.

"I could use that!" Buzz cried.

Whap! Suddenly, he was attacked by a new Buzz space ranger. Although he struggled, Andy's toy was overpowered and imprisoned inside a box on the shelf. He began trying to escape right away

New Buzz thought Andy's toys were on a mission to defeat the Emperor Zurg, so he joined Rex and the others, who were touring the store in a toy sports car.

The toys stopped outside Al's office, where they could hear him talking on the phone. He was discussing his plan to sell Woody to a collector in Japan! They all hid in Al's briefcase as he left for home.

Once inside Al's apartment, the toys escaped from his briefcase. New Buzz rushed over to Bullseye. "We're here, Woody!" he yelled.

Andy's toys looked at New Buzz suspiciously. Then Andy's real Buzz appeared. The toys were confused!

"There's no time to explain," Andy's Buzz said to everyone. "Come on, Woody! Let's go!" But to his amazement, Woody refused.

"No," Woody said sadly. "When I'm worn out, Andy will just throw me away." He turned around and switched on the TV.

But as Woody watched a small, smiling boy on the TV screen, he realized just how much he missed Andy. "Hey, Buzz! Wait!" he shouted. But the Prospector blocked the way.

Buzz turned to help his friend, but just then Al came into the room. He scooped his valuable toys into a suitcase and took them to the airport!

"We have to get Woody!" Buzz shouted. But as they headed for the elevator, they heard an evil laugh.

"It's Zurg!" Rex gasped.

Bravely Buzz and New Buzz fought off the attack. Rex closed his eyes in panic. Then, *thwack*! His tail knocked Zurg off the roof of the elevator car. "I won! I defeated Zurg!" Rex shouted excitedly.

Andy's toys said good-bye to New Buzz and raced through the hall after Woody.

Luckily, they spotted a pizza truck nearby, and the toys jumped in. With Buzz at the steering wheel, Slinky on the pedals, Rex as navigator, and Hamm working the levers, they zigzagged their way to the airport. There, the toys ran inside, desperately looking for Al.

Al was still at the check-in desk. As his suitcase thumped onto the conveyor belt, the toys jumped up beside it.

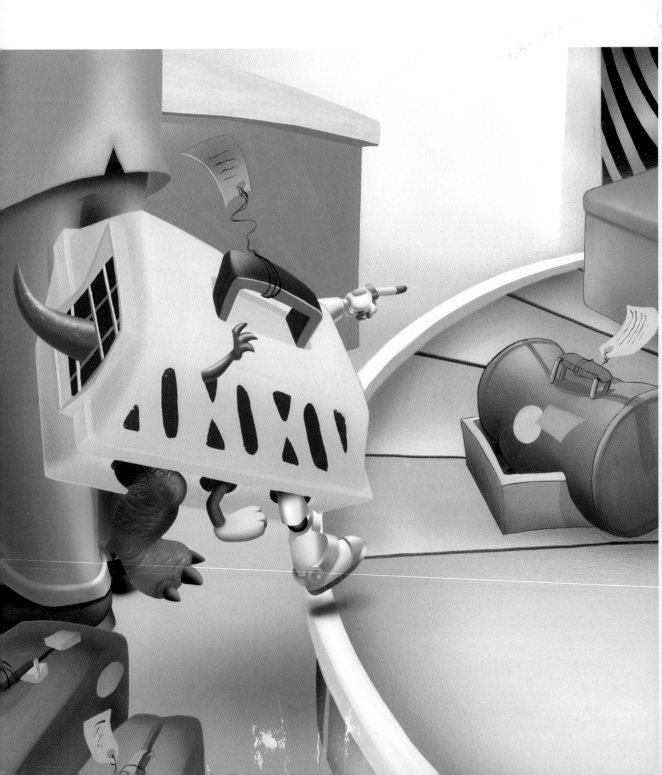

"Woody, are you in there?" Buzz called, and he opened the catch.

Pow! The Prospector came out fighting. Buzz fought back and quickly trapped him inside a backpack.

Woody and Bullseye had managed to get out of Al's suitcase, but Jessie was still trapped inside.

I'm *not* letting Jessie down! Woody thought. She deserves another chance to play with a kid who loves her.

Woody, Buzz, and Bullseye galloped after Jessie as the suitcase got closer to the plane.

Woody dived into a golf bag as it was loaded on the plane. Then he searched the bags until he found Jessie.

"Oh, Woody, I knew you'd come!" she cried.

"We're not out of here yet," Woody said grimly. "And we haven't much time left!"

They felt the plane begin to move toward the runway.

Woody tried to help Jessie down, but his weak arm gave way. . . .

"Help!" she cried, as she fell toward the plane's wheel.

Thinking quickly, Woody used his string as a lasso and pulled Jessie up safely.

At the same moment, Bullseye and Buzz galloped toward them. "Jump! Woody! Jump!" called Buzz.

Holding Jessie tightly, Woody dropped onto Bullseye's back.

Later that day, Andy arrived back home. He was happy to be back. And he was even more pleased to see Bullseye and Jessie with the other toys on his bed! He started to play with them at once.

The toys all smiled. They were safe at last—back in Andy's room!

Marlin was a clownfish, but that didn't mean he thought life was very funny. All he did was worry about his little son, Nemo. Marlin had lost his wife and more than four hundred eggs in a ruthless barracuda attack. Nemo had survived, but he had one damaged fin. Marlin was determined that no harm would ever come to his only son.

Nemo was a fun-loving fish who was looking forward to starting school and making new friends. But Marlin was so protective he didn't even like Nemo going beyond their sea anemone home.

"What's the one thing we have to remember about the ocean?" he asked Nemo sternly.

"It's not safe," Nemo said with a sigh.

On the first day of school, all the
kids went on an outing to the edge
of the reef. Nemo had made
some new friends and they
sneaked off together, daring
each other to swim out into the
open sea. Nemo was nervous and
didn't venture very far, but it was
way too far for Marlin, who was
hovering nearby.

"You think you can
do these things but
you just can't, Nemo!"
Marlin yelled, rushing over.
Nemo decided to prove
him wrong. While his dad was
distracted, the little fish swam out
toward a boat anchored overhead.

Brave little Nemo had made it all the way to the boat when disaster struck—a scuba diver grabbed him!

"Daddy, help me!" Nemo yelled as he was scooped up in a net.

"Coming, Nemo!" cried Marlin. There was nothing he wouldn't do to save his precious son. But Marlin couldn't catch up with the divers. Their boat sped off so fast that a diver's mask fell overboard.

Marlin set out to find Nemo. A beautiful regal blue tang fish named Dory offered to help him, but unfortunately she had a short-term-memory problem.

"I forget things almost instantly," she explained and promptly forgot who Marlin was. "Er . . . can I help you?" she asked.

Marlin sighed and turned to go, only to come face-to-face with a shark!

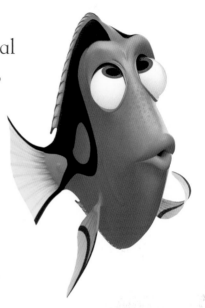

The shark was called Bruce. He was trying to be a vegetarian.
Bruce wanted the fish to meet his like-minded buddies, so they
could prove their motto: "Fish are friends, not food!"

Dory, as enthusiastic as she was forgetful, thought the whole
thing was a great idea. Marlin, who was totally terrified, did
not!

The sharks held their meetings in a wrecked submarine.

"It has been three weeks since my last fish," Bruce told his friends proudly.

Always eager, Dory joined in. "I don't think I've ever eaten a fish," she said.

Just then, Marlin spotted the mask belonging to the diver who had taken Nemo! Dory wanted to show it to the sharks but Marlin didn't. As they tussled with the mask, Dory bumped her nose and it bled a little. Bruce got a sudden craving for a fish dinner!

After a struggle, the two fish escaped with the mask in tow.
But disaster struck when Dory accidentally dropped the mask
into a deep ocean trench.

As they swam down after it, Marlin and Dory were attracted
to a bright light in the deep, dark water. It turned out to be the
glowing antenna of a scary anglerfish just waiting to pounce!

While Marlin fought the fish, its light revealed an address written on the diver's mask. Luckily, Dory remembered that she could read!

"42 Wallaby Way, Sydney," she read.

Using the mask to trap the anglerfish against a rock, Marlin and Dory set off in search of the East Australian Current, which would take them to Sydney—and Nemo!

Meanwhile, Nemo found himself in a dentist's fish tank in Sydney, where he met Bubbles, Peach, Jacques, Bloat, Deb, Flo, Gurgle, and their leader, Gill.

Poor Nemo soon discovered how small the tank was. He could hardly swim any distance without hitting the sides. Worse still, Nemo learned that he was going to be given to the dentist's niece, a terrifying girl named Darla. The tank fish were worried.

"She's a fish killer," whispered Peach.

Later that night, the fish told Nemo he could join their gang. "If," Bloat said, "you are able to swim through the Ring of Fire!"

It sounded scary, but really it was just a trail of bubbles floating out of a fake volcano. Nemo bravely made it through the bubbles. Now he was one of the gang!

"We're gonna help him escape," Gill said. Then he told his friends about how they could *all* escape the tank.

Back in the ocean, Marlin and Dory were in trouble. They had swum into a forest of jellyfish. They both got badly stung, and passed out.

Sometime later, Marlin awoke to find himself on the back of a sea turtle named Crush. Marlin told Crush about Nemo. "We need to find the East Australian Current," he said.

"You're riding it, dude!" Crush laughed as they whizzed along with the other turtles.

Tales of Marlin's adventures were spreading far and wide. Nigel, a friendly pelican who knew the Tank Gang, eventually heard the stories and rushed to tell Nemo the incredible news.

Nemo was amazed. He had always thought his dad was a bit of a scaredy-fish. The thought that he was battling his way to Sydney made the little fish proud.

Filled with new hope of returning to his ocean home, Nemo was determined to escape. He listened carefully to Gill's plan, then he took a pebble from the bottom of the tank and bravely swam up the filter pipe and jammed the tank's filter.

Thanks to Nemo, the water inside the tank gradually became green and filthy. Soon the dentist would have to take the fish out of the tank to clean it. Then they simply had to wait to be put in bags on the counter. From there, they could roll out of the window into the harbor below.

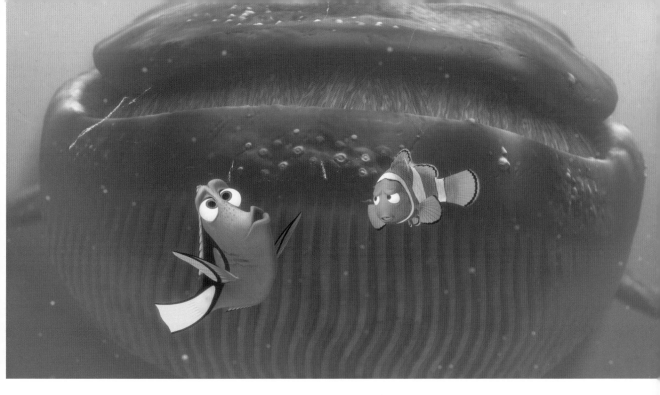

Back in the ocean, Marlin and Dory said good-bye to the turtles, but soon found themselves swallowed up inside the mouth of a massive whale.

"It's okay, I speak Whale," Dory assured Marlin. "He either said we should move to the back of his throat, or he wants a root-beer float," she translated.

It turned out the whale was only giving the two little fish a lift. They were soon squirted out of the whale's blowhole, right into Sydney Harbor!

Marlin and Dory nearly ended up as breakfast for a hungry pelican, but the two fish struggled so hard that he soon spat them out onto the dock. Luckily, Nigel rushed to their rescue.

"Hop inside my mouth if you want to live," he whispered to Marlin and Dory.

The weary fish realized they could either be eaten by a seagull, or trust the big pelican. Scooping them up, Nigel flew toward the dentist's office.

Meanwhile, the dentist had cleaned the tank water with a fancy new automated cleaner—while the fish were still in the tank! The escape plan was ruined.

Despite their efforts to save him, Nemo was soon lifted out of the tank and plopped into a bag. Darla had arrived. Nemo had one last chance—he played dead, hoping that he would get flushed down the toilet and out into the ocean.

Nigel stumbled through the window with Marlin and Dory just in time to see Nemo floating upside down in the plastic bag. The dentist quickly shooed Nigel away, but in the commotion he dropped Nemo. The bag burst open.

"I get a fishy!" squealed Darla as she reached out to grab him.

But the Tank Gang had a plan.
They launched Gill out of
the tank.

"Tell your dad I said hi!"
Gill yelled as he catapulted
the startled Nemo into the
sink.

Once back in the tank,
Gill reassured his friends.
"Don't worry," he said. "All
drains lead to the ocean."

Nigel flew back to the harbor and dropped Marlin and Dory in the water. Marlin thought he had lost Nemo for good and swam off to be on his own.

But then Dory found Nemo. She couldn't believe her eyes when she realized who the little orange clownfish was! Together, they swam after Marlin as fast as Nemo's little fins would let them.

There was a joyful reunion as Marlin realized how strong his son was and how overprotective he had been. He and Nemo had both learned that life was an adventure to be lived to the fullest.

Meanwhile, the Tank Gang were having an adventure of their own. They had finally made their escape. Now they just had to find a way to get out of the bags!

All the children of the world knew that nighttime was when scary monsters visited them through their closet doors. What they didn't know was that the monsters were just doing their jobs collecting children's screams, which provided power to their monster world.

The monsters worked for Mr. Waternoose, president of Monsters, Inc., the largest scream-processing factory in the world. James P. Sullivan, the number one Scarer at Monsters, Inc., and his assistant, Mike Wazowski, always collected the most screams.

But being a Scarer was a dangerous job.

"Never let a kid through one of our doors! Contact with children is deadly!" Mr. Waternoose warned new recruits.

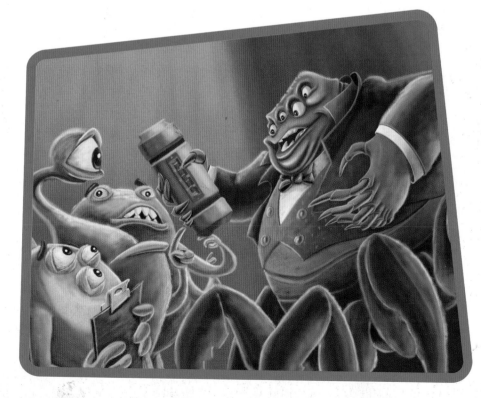

Since there was a scream shortage, Mike and Sulley walked through Monstropolis to work.

Mike went to see Roz, the sluglike monster dispatcher at Monsters, Inc., who scolded him for forgetting to file his paperwork. Then, Mike went to the Scare Floor to prepare for work. As the assistants brought in the closet doors, the Scarers entered the Scare Floor.

Randall, who wasn't a very nice monster, wanted to beat Sulley and become the top Scarer.

"May the best monster win!" said Sulley.

"I plan to!" said Randall, spitefully.

The monsters raced in and out of children's rooms, scaring kids and collecting screams.

"Emergency! We have a 2319!" cried the floor manager, as a monster returned with a child's sock on its back. A child's possession was nearly as deadly to monsters as the child itself.

The Scare Floor had to be shut down and decontaminated by the Child Detection Agency, the CDA.

With work over for the day, Mike went to meet his girlfriend, Celia, the company's beautiful receptionist. He was taking her to dinner to celebrate her birthday.

But he'd forgotten to file his paperwork. Sulley offered to help him and went back to the Scare Floor. While he was there, he accidentally let a human girl into the monster world!

After several failed attempts to return the dangerous child, Sulley hid her inside a sports bag. Then he went to find Mike, who was on his date with Celia. But the child escaped, scaring all the monsters in the restaurant!

As agents from the CDA swarmed overhead in helicopters, Sulley and Mike grabbed the girl and escaped to their apartment.

Inside, Mike tripped and fell. The little girl giggled, making all the lights flash brightly and then go out. This puzzled Sulley.

Sulley and Mike named the little girl "Boo," and put her to bed for the night.

In the morning, Sulley decided to try to put Boo back through her door again.

Dressing her in a monster disguise, he and Mike took her with them to work. The Monsters, Inc. lobby was crawling with CDA agents.

While Mike tried to find the key to her door, Boo played with Sulley.

Mike returned to find Sulley and Boo playing hide-and-seek, just as Randall and his assistant, Fungus, arrived.

"Shhh!" whispered Sulley, and they hid just in time.

"When I find whoever let that kid out . . ." muttered Randall.

"This is very bad," said Mike. It seemed that sneaky, mean Randall had had plans for Boo!

But once again Boo escaped . . . and Sulley rushed off to look for her.

Once Mike was alone, Randall cornered him.

"Where's the kid? It's here in the factory, isn't it?" he growled.

Terrified, Mike admitted everything.

Randall told Mike to return Boo to her door while the Scare Floor was empty—at lunchtime.

Once they had found Boo with some little monsters in the company day care, Sulley and Mike headed back to the Scare Floor. But Sulley didn't trust Randall.

Frustrated, Mike opened Boo's door and went into the room to prove everything was safe.

Mike jumped on the bed, pretending to be Boo. Suddenly, he was trapped inside a box!

Hiding with Boo, Sulley watched as Randall left the room, carrying the box with Mike inside it!

Sulley and Boo followed them into a secret laboratory. Randall strapped Mike to a machine that extracted screams from children.

But Sulley secretly unplugged the machine and rescued Mike. Then they ran to find Mr. Waternoose, and tell him about Randall's evil plot.

But as they were trying to tell Mr. Waternoose what had happened, he grabbed Boo, opened a door . . . and pushed Mike and Sulley through it. Mr. Waternoose was in on Randall's plan!

Mike and Sulley had been banished to the human world. They found themselves on a snowy mountain with the Abominable Snowman—the Yeti!

When the Yeti told them about a nearby village, Sulley had an idea.

He made a sleigh out of bits and pieces he found in the Yeti's cave. When Mike refused to go with him, Sulley sped down the mountain alone.

Charging into a child's bedroom and through the closet door, Sulley entered the monster world and raced toward Randall's secret lab, where he found Boo strapped to the machine. Sulley ripped the machine apart and rescued Boo.

Luckily, Mike had decided to follow his old friend after all, and helped them to escape.

Running to the Scare Floor, Mike explained to Celia what had been happening.

While Celia caused a distraction, Mike and Sulley found Boo's door. But Randall was close behind!

Randall grabbed Boo and then tried to loosen Sulley's grip on the door so he would fall. Suddenly, Boo pulled Randall's head back.

Then Sulley threw Randall through an open door and shredded it so that he could never return!

With a look of pride, Sulley lifted Boo up into the air and laughed, "You did it Boo! You beat him!"

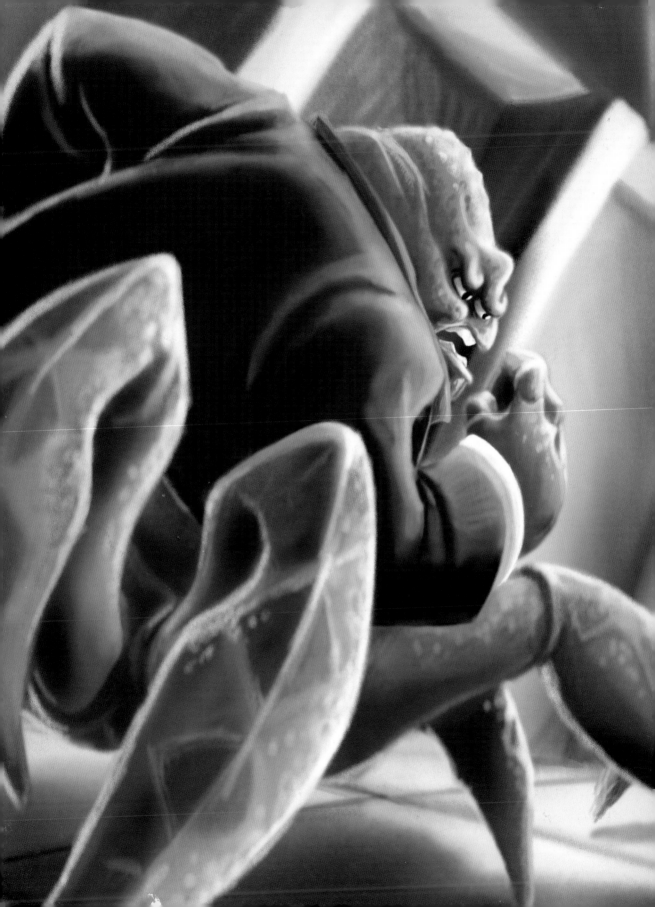

Now it was time to escape from Mr. Waternoose. "I'll kidnap a thousand children before I let this company die!" he gasped.

The CDA, who had heard everything, arrested Mr. Waternoose, then announced the arrival of their boss . . . who turned out to be Roz! She had been working as an undercover agent for the CDA all along!

Roz gave Mike and Sulley five minutes to say good-bye to Boo. Then the little girl was sent home. Her door was shredded so that no monster could ever enter her room again.

Later, when Sulley explained to everyone how Boo's laughter created more power than her screams, Monsters, Inc. was turned into a laughter factory. Sulley became the president, and profits soared.

Sulley still missed Boo. In fact, he was thinking about her when Mike arrived with a surprise for him.

Mike had put Boo's shredded door back together! Once the final piece was in place, Sulley walked into Boo's room. The little girl grinned. Sulley smiled at her. At last they were reunited!